To Stephanie Morgan, the incredible children's librarian at Kingston Library
—JD & DS

Agent Lion
Copyright © 2020 by Jacky Davis and David Soman
All rights reserved. Manufactured in China.
No part of this book may be used or reproduced in any manner whatsoever without written permission except in the case of brief quotations embodied in critical articles and reviews. For information address HarperCollins Children's Books, a division of HarperCollins Publishers, 195 Broadway, New York, NY 10007.
www.harpercollinschildrens.com

Library of Congress Control Number: 2018964873
ISBN 978-0-06-286917-3

The artist used pen and ink and watercolor to create the illustrations for this book.
Typography by Chelsea C. Donaldson
19 20 21 22 23 SCP 10 9 8 7 6 5 4 3 2 1
❖
First Edition

AGENT LION

DAVID SOMAN AND JACKY DAVIS

HARPER

An Imprint of HarperCollinsPublishers

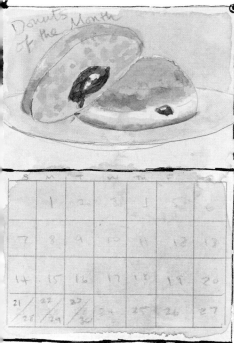

Agent Lion was hard at work.

When suddenly . . .

The phone rang. It was Ms. Chief from headquarters, and since Ms. Chief was THE CHIEF, it had to be a very important call.

"Agent Lion," she said,

"Ms. Flamingo's cat, Fluffy, is missing! And it's up to you to find him."

Agent Lion knew that he was the very best detective for the job.

He buckled his helmet, hopped on his bicycle,
and was on his way.

He took the absolutely most direct route.

THE FLAMINGO RESIDENCE

PiyyaTown

POPCORN PALACE
·MOVIES·

Best Burgers

Scoops Ice Cream

Two hours later Agent Lion was knocking on Ms. Flamingo's door.

"Hello, Ms. Flamingo. I am Agent Lion from the Super Detective Agents Agency, and I am here to find your cat. First, I will need a description of Fluffy. Does Fluffy have a trunk?"

"No, Fluffy does not have a trunk," said Ms. Flamingo.

"I see," said Agent Lion. "Does he have antlers?"
"No," she replied. "Fluffy is a cat!"

"Wings?" asked Agent Lion.
Ms. Flamingo was getting frustrated.

FLIPPETY FLIPPETY FLIP

"This is Fluffy!" she said. "Fluffy looks like a cat because HE IS A CAT!"
Now that Agent Lion was clear on what Fluffy looked like, he needed to start looking for clues.

First, he checked the living room.

Then, he checked the bathroom.

"Now I must check the refrigerator," said Agent Lion.

Ms. Flamingo was confused. "Agent Lion, why on earth are you looking for Fluffy in the refrigerator?"

"I am not looking for Fluffy," he said. "I am looking for jelly donuts!"

It had been a tiring morning, and Agent Lion needed a snack.

Once Agent Lion concluded that Fluffy was not in the apartment, he thought to look on the roof, since everyone knows that cats like to fly kites.

"No one move!" said Agent Lion, coming to a halt. "I think we've found him."

"Agent Lion," said Ms. Flamingo, "that is a pigeon."

"Ah, but look closely," said Agent Lion. "That pigeon could be Fluffy in disguise."

Ms. Flamingo was trying to be patient. "Agent Lion, cats do not wear pigeon disguises," she explained.

TAP
TAP
TAP

Agent Lion decided it was time to move on to the next stage of the investigation. "Let's interview our first witness!"

They went to Mr. Wombat's apartment and knocked on the door.

"Hello," said Agent Lion. "We are looking for Fluffy. Have you seen him?"

"No," answered Mr. Wombat, "I have not seen Fluffy. I've been here baking a cake."

Agent Lion's eyes widened. "A cake, you say? I love cake! Is it a birthday cake? An ice-cream cake? Is it my favorite, a jelly-donut cake?"

"Come on, Agent Lion," urged Ms. Flamingo. "We must keep searching for Fluffy."

"Wait. I have one more very important question," said Agent Lion.

"What time will the cake be ready?"

Agent Lion and Ms. Flamingo walked down to the next floor and stopped at a suspiciously quiet door.

"Cats love quiet," said Agent Lion. "Maybe Fluffy is here!"

DING-DONG! DING-DONG!

"Shhhhh!" said Ms. Hippo. "My babies are asleep."

"Sorry to interrupt you," said Agent Lion. "I am looking for Fluffy. May I look around?"

"Okay," agreed Ms. Hippo. "But you have to be very quiet."

"Do not worry," whispered Agent Lion. "I am the best at being quiet."

"Oh, look, a tuba! Cats can't resist a good polka!"

The babies blinked their eyes, and then . . .

"WAAAAAAA! WAAAAAA!" they cried.

"Oh no! You woke the babies!"

"Agent Lion, I think it's time for us to go," said Ms. Flamingo.

"What? I can't hear you!" said Agent Lion.

"I said, we should leave!" Ms. Flamingo yelled.

"Yes!" Agent Lion yelled back. "It's much too noisy in here for a cat."

Agent Lion thought it was time to get to the bottom of things. They took the elevator down to the lobby. It was busy with everyone coming and going, but they did not see Fluffy.

Agent Lion decided to check the mail room.

"Cats love getting mail!" he said.

"Not here! Not here!"

"Here!"

"Have you finally found Fluffy?" asked Ms. Flamingo.

"No," replied Agent Lion. "I did not find Fluffy. But I did find my favorite magazine, *Jelly Donut Digest*."

"Agent Lion, I've had **enough!**" announced Ms. Flamingo. "The investigation is over. I am going home. You are welcome to join me for a cup of tea if you like."

Agent Lion sadly followed her back to her apartment.

Ms. Flamingo went straight to the kitchen to boil water.

Agent Lion rearranged the couch pillows.

He felt terrible and was beginning to doubt if he really was the very best detective after all.

But then the pillow said,

"PURRRRRRRRRRRRRRRR . . ."

"Wait a minute," said Agent Lion. "You are not a pillow!"

"You are Fluffy!"

"You did it, Agent Lion!" said Ms. Flamingo, skipping into the room. "You found Fluffy! How can I ever thank you enough?" she asked.

Agent Lion humbly replied, "I was just doing my job. But if you insist . . ."

"Jelly donuts do go particularly well with tea."